For my parents, my siblings and their spouses, and
Samantha, Sebastian, Jeremy and Alexander.   —*David Seow*

For Father, with whom all things are possible.
And for the child in all us.   —*L.K. Tay-Audouard*

Cultural Background

The Chinese classic *Journey to the West,* or *Monkey King* as it is
popularly known, was written by Wu Ch'eng-en (1500-1582) and
has been a favorite story for generations of Chinese around the
world. Inspired by the life of the famous monk, Xuan Zang, who
journeyed to India in search of holy Buddhist scriptures, Wu
Ch'eng-en crafted an amazing, wondrous tale with elements of
Chinese legends and folktales along with aspects of Buddhist and
Taoist mythology.

ABOUT TUTTLE
"Books to Span the East and West"

Our core mission at Tuttle Publishing is to create books which bring
people together one page at a time. Tuttle was founded in 1832
in the small New England town of Rutland, Vermont (USA). Our
fundamental values remain as strong today as they were then—to
publish best-in-class books informing the English-speaking world
about the countries and peoples of Asia. The world has become
a smaller place today and Asia's economic, cultural and political
influence has expanded, yet the need for meaningful dialogue and
information about this diverse region has never been greater. Since
1948, Tuttle has been a leader in publishing books on the cultures,
arts, cuisines, languages and literatures of Asia. Our authors and
photographers have won numerous awards and Tuttle has published thousands of books on subjects ranging from martial arts to
paper crafts. We welcome you to explore the wealth of information
available on Asia at www.tuttlepublishing.com.

Published by Tuttle Publishing,
an imprint of Periplus Editions (HK) Ltd.

www.tuttlepublishing.com

Text © 2005 Periplus Editions (HK) Ltd
Illustrations © 2005 L.K. Tay-Audouard

LCC Card No: 2004110836
ISBN 978-0-8048-4840-4

First printing, 2005
Printed in Hong Kong
20 19 18 17   5 4 3 2 1   1611EP

Distributed by:

North America, Latin America & Europe
Tuttle Publishing
364 Innovation Drive, North Clarendon
VT 05759-9436 U.S.A.
Tel: (802) 773-8930
Fax: (802) 773-6993
info@tuttlepublishing.com
www.tuttlepublishing.com

Asia Pacific
Berkeley Books Pte. Ltd.
61 Tai Seng Avenue # 02-12
Singapore 534167
Tel: (65) 6280-1330
Fax: (65) 6280-6290
inquiries@periplus.com.sg
www.periplus.com

Japan
Tuttle Publishing
Yaekari Building, 3rd Floor
5-4-12 Osaki, Shinagawa-ku
Tokyo 141 0032
Tel: (81) 3 5437-0171
Fax: (81) 3 5437-0755
sales@tuttle.co.jp; www.tuttle.co.jp

The MONKEY KING
A Classic Chinese Tale for Children

by David Seow

illustrations by L.K. Tay-Audouard

TUTTLE Publishing

Tokyo | Rutland, Vermont | Singapore

Long ago, there was great chaos and disorder in China. People were filled with jealousy, greed and anger. **The Jade Emperor**, ruler of the Heavens, summoned his court. "Shall I send a great bolt of lightning to destroy these ungrateful earthlings?" he asked.

2

Guan Yin, the Goddess of Mercy, quietly advised, "Your Majesty, **there is still hope.** The Lord Buddha has written scriptures that show the way to kindness, peace and harmony. These holy scriptures are in India. If we can bring them to China, they will guide the people."

The Jade Emperor agreed. He commanded Guan Yin to find someone brave and noble enough to undertake this quest.

After searching high and low, Guan Yin found a monk with a pure heart. She told him about the Jade Emperor's request, but she also warned him: "Finding the scriptures will not be easy! You will face many dangers. But you will have loyal friends to help you."

The monk replied, "My life is devoted to peace and knowledge. I gladly accept this challenge!"

Guan Yin presented him with **a priest's robe, a golden bowl and a magnificent white horse.** She named him **Tripitaka— The Great Scripture Seeker**—and bid him a safe journey.

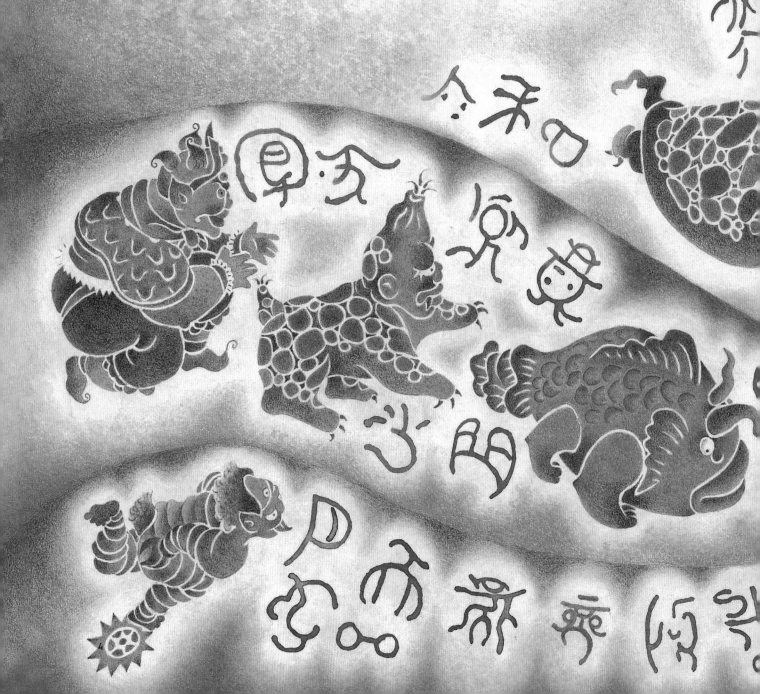

After riding for several days, Tripitaka passed the Five Elements Mountain. The road was rocky and strange demons lay in wait to ambush travelers. Bravely, Tripitaka rode into the forest. Bamboos creaked in the cold wind as he passed. KRIIIK! KRAAAK! BOOOM!

Suddenly a voice rang out, "AH... HA-HA-HA!!" Tripitaka quickly dismounted and peered into the undergrowth.

"HEE-HEE-HEE!!" came the voice again, this time louder and closer.

Then someone or something grabbed his ankle! "AI-YEE!" he cried! Looking down, Tripitaka saw a furry paw holding his ankle and a grinning monkey's face peering up at him. "Did you make those noises?" Tripitaka demanded.

"Yes! HE-E HA-A HO-O!" cackled the monkey as he released Tripitaka's ankle.

"What a scare you gave me! Who are you, and what are you doing under this mountain?" asked the monk.

"I am the Monkey King, Great Sage Equal to Heaven, with fantastic powers of transformation! I was cast out of Heaven for stealing food from the Jade Emperor's table. I have been under this mountain ever since," explained Monkey.

"That seems like a very harsh punishment," Tripitaka said, puzzled.

"I'm sure the Jade Emperor would have forgiven me for eating his food— if only I had stopped there," Monkey's eyes sparkled with mischief.

"**Oh, the wonderful foods I ate that day**—wing of flying fish, tail of

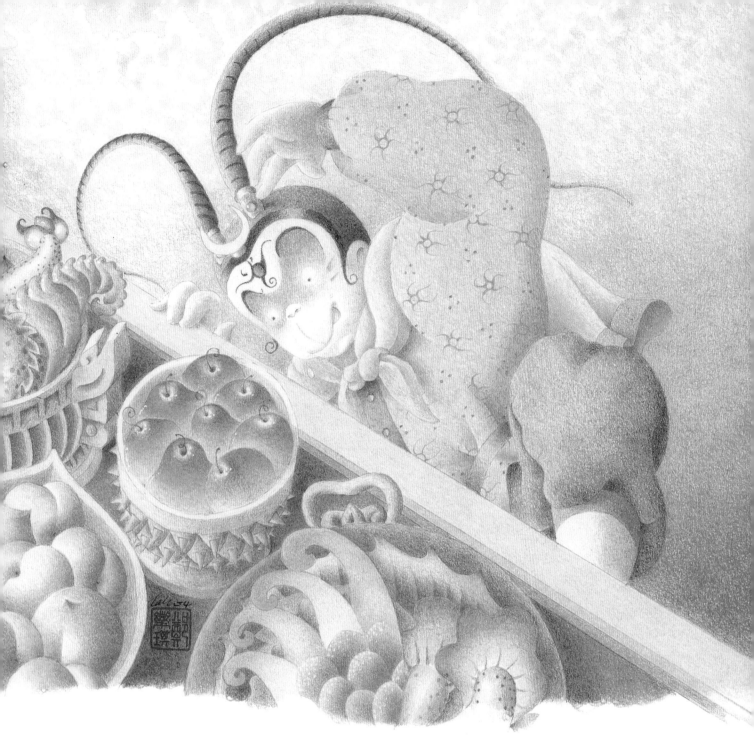

dragon, rainbow eggs of jeweled carp, and much more! But most delicious of all
was the **Elixir of Immortality** which belongs to the Emperor and only he can
drink it," Monkey continued. "At first, I took just a sip. But ah, it was heavenly!
Then I gulped it all down. Furious, the Jade Emperor imprisoned me here. To
redeem myself, I must find the Great Scripture Seeker and help him."

"But I am the Great Scripture Seeker!" Tripitaka exclaimed.

"What luck! You have the power to free me!" Monkey screeched with glee.

Tripitaka now remembered Guan Yin's words. Could this monkey be someone to help him on his quest? He looked skyward and cried out, "If Monkey is meant to join me, please release him!"

In an instant, the mountain crumbled and Monkey was freed. He shook off the dust and picked up his wooden staff.

"Do you really have magical powers?" Tripitaka asked him.

"I can transform myself in a thousand ways. One hair of mine can become an army of monkeys! **I can hop on a cloud** and circle the globe in the blink of an eye!" As he said this, Monkey leapt onto a cloud and disappeared. An instant later, he reappeared in the branches of a tree. Then he vanished again—and reappeared sitting on a rock next to Tripitaka.

"You are very fast," said Tripitaka. "You may join me on my quest as long as you behave yourself!" As Tripitaka said this, Monkey took aim and hurled his magical staff in the direction of the startled monk.

"What are you doing?" Tripitaka exclaimed, as **the staff whizzed past** his head. When he turned around, however, he saw a fierce tiger about to pounce on him. The staff struck the tiger and killed it instantly.

"Monkey, You saved my life! THANK YOU!" said the grateful monk.

Tripitaka and Monkey continued
on their way together and soon
entered the Great Bamboo Forest, where
giant ogres lay in wait. Suddenly, a scream
pierced the air and a snorting pig-like creature leapt out
from the bushes. In his mouth was a big red bean bun.

"M-mmm, Pigsy loves red bean buns!" sniffled the creature.

Monkey rushed forward to attack him, but Pigsy countered with his rake.
They fought so fiercely that the bamboos shuddered and even the giant
ogres were frightened! "Let me finish you off and be on my way with the
Great Scripture Seeker!" Monkey shouted.

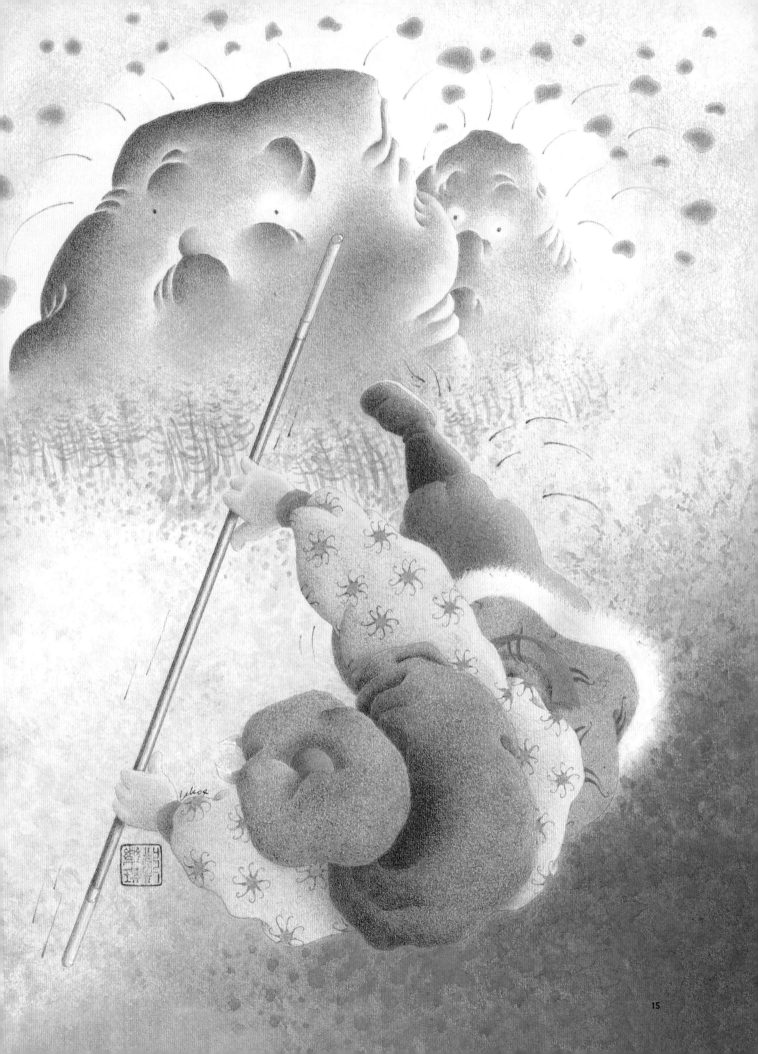

"The Great Scripture Seeker? Is he here?" squealed Pigsy.
"Can you take me to him? He is my only hope! I
wasn't always like this. I was once **Keeper of
the Heavenly Garden** of the Jade Empress.
Oh, her beauty! One day, I plucked up my
courage and declared my love to her. But
she screamed, and the Jade Emperor
transformed me into this ugly pig.
My only hope of salvation is to
meet the Great Scripture Seeker."
"I'll take you to my Master.
He will decide." Monkey declared.
When Tripitaka heard his story,
he realized that Pigsy too might
be helpful to their cause. So
the three of them agreed to
journey on together.

After several days, they came to the
Great Sandy Bottom River. It was strangely
silent. Not a soul could be seen.

"I hear that a horrible monster lives
in this river. It destroys everything.
How can we cross?" Pigsy asked.

"All I need to do is leap on a cloud!"
Monkey boasted.

"What about us?" Pigsy said. "Can you
transform yourself into a boat and carry us across?"

"No silly, I can only turn myself into living things."

"Well, that's not very helpful, is it? Aren't you the
Great Sage Equal to Heaven?" snorted Pigsy.

"Maybe you can float across on your huge stomach!
HEE-HE-EE-HA-HA-AA!" countered Monkey.

As they were arguing, a large creature with
spiky red hair rose from the river depths. Before
the others noticed him, **the monster snatched
Tripitaka's horse** and quickly disappeared
into the water.

Monkey plunged into the river after him. But the monster disappeared into **a dark cave guarded by sentries.**

"Stop! Return my Master's horse!" Monkey commanded.

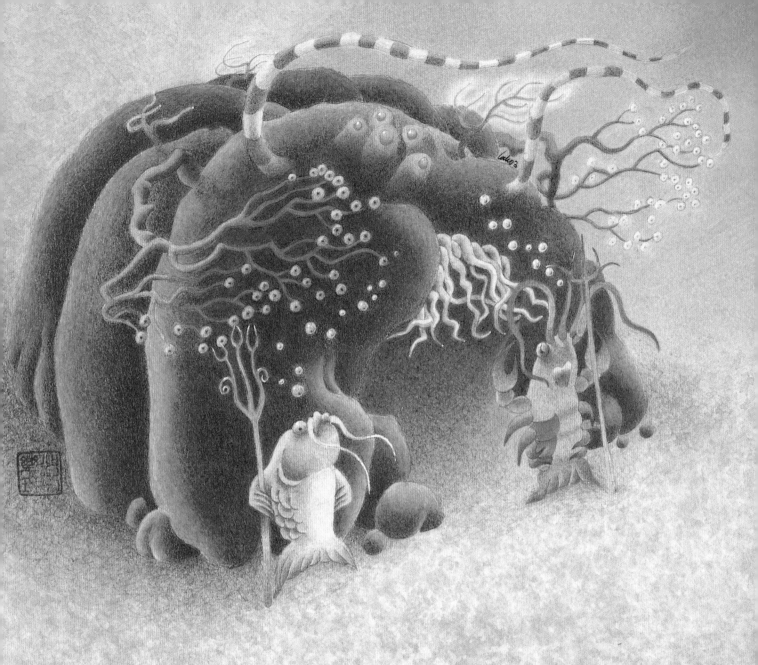

Bubbles of laughter escaped from the cave. Immediately, a hoard of fish and lobster soldiers appeared. Monkey quickly plucked a hair from his head and a thousand monkeys materialized to overpower the underwater army.

"Looks like I'll have to destroy this monkey myself!" said the monster. But when he emerged from the cave, there was no Monkey in sight.

"Ha! The coward has fled." Just then, a large beetle jumped on the monster's back and bit him very hard. "OWWWWW!" It was Monkey in disguise! With a howl, the monster shot out of the water and landed on the river bank.

Pigsy soon joined the fight. He and Monkey were so busy fighting the monster that they didn't notice a giant eagle who swooped down on Tripitaka and carried him away.

"H-E-L-P M-E-eee!" Tripitaka's voice trailed away from above.

"Oh no, that eagle has kidnapped our Master, the Great Scripture Seeker!" Pigsy cried.

The monster was stunned. "Is that really the Great Scripture Seeker? In that case, please let me help you!"

Shocked, Monkey and Pigsy lowered their weapons and asked the monster to explain who he was.

"My name is Sandy". said the monster. "I was once the Jade Emperor's cook.

24

Whenever he was not looking, I would perform **juggling acts with his priceless dishes.** One day, I lost my balance and broke his porcelains into a thousand pieces. As punishment, the Jade Emperor turned me into this ugly monster. The only way I can escape is to find the Great Scripture Seeker and help him."

Monkey and Pigsy said, "We will take you to our Master. He will decide."

So Monkey and Pigsy let Sandy join them on their rescue mission. Monkey transformed himself into a giant falcon and Pigsy and Sandy hopped on his back. They chased the eagle, but as they approached, a **flock of eagles attacked them.** Fighting furiously, Monkey, Pigsy and Sandy drove them away. They tracked the eagle to a large, dark cave at the top of the mountain, and the three of them peered inside. "Master, are you there?" Their voices echoed. "MA-A-ASTER!"

"I'm here, in this basket filled with boulders," Tripitaka shouted. "Help me out. QUICKLY!"

Just then, **the eagle returned!** With its huge claws, it flung Pigsy and Sandy into the basket. Monkey transformed himself into a bird and flew off, and the eagle gave chase.

In the basket, Sandy quickly explained to Tripitaka who he was. "In heaven, I could change objects into anything I desired. Now that I'm here to help the Great Scripture Seeker, maybe my powers are restored. Let me turn this basket into something breakable."

Sandy tapped the basket and it magically turned into a porcelain bowl. As he did that, however, Pigsy noticed that the boulders were actually giant eggs, and baby eagles were hatching from them.

Hearing this, the eagle stopped
chasing Monkey and
returned to its nest. As it
entered the cave, Pigsy swung his
rake and shattered the bowl. Shards
flew in every direction, piercing the
eagle's body and killing it instantly.

Monkey turned himself into a falcon again and transported Tripitaka, Pigsy and Sandy back to safety down below.

That evening, Sandy cooked a delicious meal for the four of them. He turned **pebbles into fruits, twigs into chopsticks, leaves into plates,** and prepared a special dish of roast eagle hatchling!

As they ate, each gave his own version of the day's events.

"I did an amazing job rescuing our Master," said Sandy.

"You?? I smashed the nest!" Pigsy boasted.

"But I turned it into porcelain, ..." countered Sandy.

"Hey, what about me? I lured the eagle away. I'm the real hero!" Monkey cried.

"ENOUGH!" Tripitaka commanded. "Each of you played your part in rescuing me. But if we're going to find the Lord Buddha's scriptures, we must work together. Can I count on you?"

Monkey, Pigsy and Sandy frowned but finally agreed.

"We can't promise we won't argue, but we'll try not to do it very often," Monkey offered.

"We want to help you find the scriptures and restore peace to China," said Sandy.

"We all wish to make up for our bad behavior and impress the Jade Emperor," Pigsy added.

So, the three friends pledged to work together to protect Tripitaka on his long and dangerous journey to India and back. They faced many incredible adventures along the way—but they became good friends and were loyal to each other to the end.